Hannah
and the
Whistling
Teakettle

A RICHARD JACKSON BOOK

Hannah
and the
Whistling
Teakettle

story by

Mindy Warshaw Skolsky

pictures by

Diane Palmisciano

DK
Ink

DORLING KINDERSLEY PUBLISHING, INC.

To my wonderful grandson,
Zachary Metz,
and my wonderful editor,
Dick Jackson
—M. W. S.

For my mother
—D. P.

A Richard Jackson Book

Dorling Kindersley Publishing, Inc., 95 Madison Avenue, New York, New York 10016
Visit us on the World Wide Web at http://www.dk.com

Dorling Kindersley books are available at special discounts for bulk purchases for sales promotions or premiums.
Special editions, including personalized covers, excerpts of existing guides, and corporate imprints can be created in
large quantities for specific needs. For more information, contact Special Markets Dept., Dorling Kindersley
Publishing, Inc., 95 Madison Avenue, New York, New York 10016; fax: (800) 600-9098

Library of Congress Cataloging-in-Publication Data
Skolsky, Mindy Warshaw.
Hannah and the whistling teakettle / Mindy Warshaw Skolsky ; illustrated by
Diane Palmisciano. — 1st ed.
p.   cm.
"A Richard Jackson book"
Summary: When she goes to visit her grandparents in the Bronx, Hannah wonders
if her grandmother will consider the whistling teakettle Hannah is bringing
a necessity worth keeping when it helps to foil a robbery.
ISBN 0-7894-2602-1
[1. Grandparents—Fiction.   2. Gifts—Fiction.]   I. Palmisciano, Diane, ill.   II. Title.
PZ7.S62836Hamf 2000 [E]—dc21 99-41079 CIP
Book design by Jennifer Browne.
The illustrations for this book were created using oil pastels.
The text of this book is set in 18 point Bembo.
Printed and bound in U.S.A.

First Edition, 2000
2 4 6 8 10 9 7 5 3 1

Once there was a girl named Hannah. She lived with her mother and father in a little village between a mountain and a river.

Several miles down the river, on the other side of the George Washington Bridge, was New York City. There, in a part of the city called the Bronx, lived Hannah's grandmother and grandfather.

One day in early spring, when the pussy willows outside Hannah's windows were like soft gray velvet and yellow-green buds were popping out on all the trees and birds were flying back from the south and weaving in and out through the branches, Hannah decided she would like to travel, too.

She said to her mother and father, "I think I'm big enough to go to New York City and visit Grandma and Grandpa all by myself."

Her mother called Hannah's grandmother and grandfather on the telephone, and Hannah heard her mother
say, "Hello, Mama. Hannah would like to come visit
you all by herself. Could Papa meet her bus at
the bridge?"

And Hannah heard her grandmother
say, "Why not?"

So Hannah packed her suitcase,
and her mother and father
walked her to the bus station.

Along the way they stopped in a store to buy a present for Hannah to take to her grandmother.

Hannah's grandmother never kept presents. Whatever they brought her, like the furry bedroom slippers they had brought the last time they visited, or the waffle iron the time before that, Hannah's grandmother said the same thing: "Thank you very much, but it's not a necessity."

Furry feet were not a necessity. Waffles were not a necessity. Taking the present back seemed to be the only necessity.

"You pick the present this time," said Hannah's mother. "Maybe you can find something Grandma will keep."

Hannah saw many nice things,
like a shiny necklace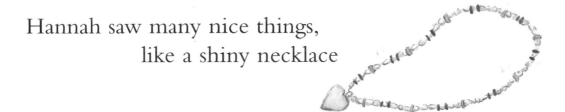

 and an ivory fan

and a tiny purse made of
colored glass beads,

but she knew her grandmother would say the same to all
of those: "Not a necessity."
Then she saw a bright silver whistling teakettle with
a little red bird on the top.

"That's just like our new kettle," said Hannah. Maybe Grandma would keep that, she thought. They drink a lot of tea. Their old kettle is so old it has bumps. And this one has a bird that whistles so Grandma won't have to keep going back to the kitchen to see if the water has boiled out.

"Maybe this is a necessity," said Hannah. "I pick this."

They paid for it and the shopkeeper put it in a bag.

Hannah got on the bus and picked a seat by the window, and the driver started the bus. She waved to her mother and father as they looked smaller and smaller, and when they finally looked like two dots in the distance, Hannah turned around and watched as the bus turned down the river road.

I'm on a bus that goes my favorite way, thought Hannah. I'm lucky! And she watched the sun sparkle on the river all the way to the George Washington Bridge and across it.

Toward the end of the bridge, Hannah began to watch for her grandfather. She saw a dot that grew bigger and bigger as they got closer and closer and then . . .

. . . turned into her life-size grandfather just as the bus slowed down.

When she saw him standing there, Hannah felt warm and happy. She jumped up, took her suitcase in one hand and the bag with the whistling teakettle in the other hand, and got to the front of the bus just as the driver opened the door.

Then Hannah stepped down and landed right in her grandfather's arms.

"Hello, my Hannah from the country!"
said Hannah's grandfather, giving her
a big hug and a kiss.

"Hello, my grandpa from the city!"
said Hannah, giving him a big hug
and a kiss right back. "Hey, let me
down—your mustache tickles!"

He took the suitcase and she kept the bag with the whistling teakettle. They held hands, and after a long subway ride, they walked past a lot of stores till Hannah saw one with a painting of an ice-cream cone in the window. "Ooh," she said. "I can't wait, Grandpa!" She ran ahead, opened the door, and rushed in.

It was the best store in the world. It was a candy store!
  Behind the counter, even better than the candy, the
sodas, the malteds, the ice-cream cones and sundaes,
and the banana splits, was Hannah's grandmother.
Hannah thought her grandmother was more
fun than anybody, even though she made
people take back presents.

Hannah ran behind the counter and her
grandmother ran forward, both at the same time.

Then Hannah's grandmother gave her a big
hug and a kiss, and Hannah gave her a big hug
and kiss right back.

Hannah's grandmother then said what she
always said when Hannah came to visit: "Come
into the back room and eat."

They went into the little room behind the candy store, and before Hannah could even take the whistling teakettle out of the bag, her grandmother had set out three bowls of chicken soup with matzo balls.

While she waited for her soup to cool, Hannah took the whistling teakettle out of the bag, held it up under the light to catch the silvery shine, and said to her grandmother, "This is your present. It's a whistling teakettle!"

"Thank you very much," said her grandmother, "but it's not a necessity."

"Grandma—sometimes when you're up front in the store, the water boils out."

"So new kettles can't boil out?"

"Not if they're whistling teakettles. The bird whistles and lets you know when the water is boiling. The bird calls you."

"Very pretty," said Hannah's grandmother, "but not a necessity."

"Grandma!" said Hannah. "I bought this *especially* for being a necessity."

Just then someone came into the candy store and Hannah's grandmother went out front.

"Grandpa," said Hannah, "can't you make Grandma keep the whistling teakettle?"

"The only present I ever got your grandmother to keep that she said was a necessity was her wedding ring," said Hannah's grandfather. "So I'd like to help you, but I don't think I can. You could show me how that whistling teakettle works, though, because it surely is an unusual thing!"

"You take the little bird off the top," said Hannah, "and you fill the kettle with water. Then you put the bird back on and light the stove, and when the tea water is ready, steam comes out of the bird's beak and the bird whistles and tells you the water is ready. You don't even have to watch the kettle."

"Amazing!" said Hannah's grandfather. "With the old kettle, we have to keep running back from the front to look. But what if we were so busy we didn't hear it? The water could boil out then."

"Grandpa," said Hannah, "when that bird whistles, you hear it. Because it whistles louder and louder till you turn it off. You'd hear it even if you were standing outside under the awning!"

When the customer left, Hannah and her grandfather
came out front. It was his penny poker night.

"See you when I get back," he said. "I'll bring something
good from the bakery. And we'll all have tea." He winked
at Hannah and whispered, "If you put the new kettle on at
ten o'clock, I could hear that bird whistling when I come
in the door."

A little while before ten o'clock, a lady named Mrs.
Beck came in for an ice-cream soda. Hannah knew she
came in every night. She was a regular.

While Hannah's grandmother was putting the ice cream
in Mrs. Beck's glass, she asked Hannah if she'd like some
ice cream, too.

"No, thank you," said Hannah. "It's almost time for
Grandpa to be home and I don't want to spoil my
appetite. I think I'll put on the water for the tea now."
She went to the back room.

"Use the old kettle," called her grandmother.

Hannah sang "My Country 'Tis of Thee" in a loud voice so she wouldn't hear. Then she filled the new kettle with water, lit the stove carefully the way her mother had taught her, put the kettle over the burner, and came back out front.

Mrs. Beck said Hannah was a nice patriotic girl. And then she said good night.

Hannah and her grandmother were cleaning up and drying glasses when two men walked into the store.

Hannah didn't recognize them—they weren't regulars. One man had a little suitcase. He went into the phone booth.

"I'd like a malted," said the other man.

"Closed," said Hannah's grandmother, pointing to the clock.

"Aw, lady," said the man, "please make me a malted. My friend has to use the phone, and I'm dying for a malted. I'll give you a quarter!"

"A quarter!" said Hannah's grandmother. "What are you, a spy to see if I raised my prices? I charge fifteen cents for malteds." She pointed to the price list on the wall. "My prices are in writing," she said. "This is an honest place."

Hannah's grandmother started to make a malted. And to prove just how honest she was, she made the two scoops of ice cream so big the malted foamed up to the top before the ice cream was even melted. But Hannah's grandmother didn't notice. Hannah saw her staring into the mirror behind the malted machine, which had begun its loud buzzing, like a bumblebee. Grandma looked so funny, Hannah looked into the mirror to see what she was looking at.

The man in the phone booth was picking at the coin box with a screwdriver and emptying out all the nickels, dimes, and quarters.

"It's worse than spies!" said Hannah's grandmother. "It's robbers!" She put her hand on the top of Hannah's head and pushed hard. Hannah landed underneath the counter right in the box of sugar cones.

"Grandma!" said Hannah. "Let me up!" Then she
got scared maybe the man would shoot her
grandmother—like in the movies—so she
pulled her grandmother down under the
counter next to her.

"What a place for a grandmother,"
said her grandmother. "I can't fit!"

The malted machine was still buzzing, and the malted was running over the counter and down to the floor. It made *slop! slop!* sounds as it landed in front of Hannah and her grandmother.

E-e-e-e!

E-e-e-e! A loud screechy noise filled the room. It was so loud it made the buzzing of the malted machine sound like a little fly instead of a bumblebee.

"Police whistle!" yelled the man in front of the counter.

E-e-e-e-e!

It got louder.

Hannah heard loud footsteps running. She heard the phone-booth door open, a sound of something dropping, lots of clattering sounds, and more footsteps running.

And

E-E-E-E-E-E-E-E

"Police! Police!" called Hannah's grandmother, getting up and running toward the front door after the two men.
E-E-E-E-E-E!

Hannah got out of the box of sugar cones and ran after her grandmother. She slipped on the malted, tripped over the open suitcase,

E-E-E-E-E

and skidded on a bunch of nickels.

E-E-E-E-E-E-E!

Hannah's grandfather came running in the front door carrying a little white box.

"What's going on here?" he yelled.

"Police!" called Hannah's grandmother. "We had a robbery."

"A robbery!" yelled Hannah's grandfather.

"A holdup of the Bell Telephone Company!" yelled back Hannah's grandmother. "Don't you hear the police whistle?"

E-E-E-E-E-E-E-E-E!

Hannah started to laugh.

"What's the joke?" asked her grandmother.

"It's not a police siren, Grandma," yelled Hannah. "It's the whistling teakettle. *The water's boiling!*"

For a minute nobody said anything. Then Hannah's grandfather turned off the malted machine and Hannah ran to the back room, and everything got quiet.

After a minute, all three of them began to laugh, and they laughed so hard they had to sit down, and even after they sat down, they still kept laughing. When they had laughed so much they couldn't laugh anymore, Hannah's grandfather mopped up the malted and picked up the coins.

Then they all went into the back room and had a glass
of tea with lemon and honey, and with her tea Hannah
had a charlotte russe, her favorite little cake.

Hannah stayed for two days. She could hardly wait
to see her mother and father, who she knew would
be waiting for her at the bus station back home
in the country.

Hannah couldn't wait to tell them
about the robbery.

But she would tell them about the robbery second. Because first she would tell them that her grandmother had *kept the whistling teakettle!*

"That little bird on the kettle maybe saved our life!" Hannah's grandmother had said. And life, she said, was a necessity!